# MR. NERVOUS

by Roger Hargreaves

## PSS!
PRICE STERN SLOAN
An Imprint of Penguin Group (USA) Inc.

Poor Mr. Nervous was frightened of everything and anything.

At the slightest little thing he would quiver and tremble and shake and turn to jelly.

So it's not really surprising to find that Mr. Nervous lives as far away from anybody as possible.

In the middle of the woods, miles and miles from anywhere.

This story begins one morning when Mr. Nervous was asleep.

It was a beautiful autumn morning. The sun was shining. The leaves on the trees had turned to a glorious red. And the wind stirred gently in the treetops.

A single leaf fell gently from the tree right outside Mr. Nervous's house and quietly brushed against his bedroom window as it fell.

Mr. Nervous awoke with a start.

"What's that terrible noise?" he cried. "Oh, heavens! The house is falling down! Oh, disaster! It's an earthquake! Oh, calamity! It's the end of the world!"

He hid under the bedclothes, trembling with fright.

After an hour, by which time he realized that his house wasn't falling down, and there wasn't an earthquake, and the world wasn't coming to an end, Mr. Nervous peeped out from under the bedclothes.

"Phew," he said. "Thank goodness for that!"

And he got up and went downstairs to make his breakfast.

Mr. Nervous poured some cornflakes out of a packet onto a plate.

Then he poured some milk onto the cornflakes.

Then he went to the cupboard to get some sugar.

*Snap! Crackle! Pop!* went the cornflakes in the milk.

"Oh, goodness gracious!" cried Mr. Nervous, diving under the kitchen table. "Oh, dear! I hear guns! Oh, calamity! It's war!"

But, of course, it wasn't.

And, of course, Mr. Nervous eventually came out from under the table and ate up all his cornflakes.

After breakfast, Mr. Nervous thought that he'd go for a walk.

He was walking through the woods that surround his house when a worm poked his head out of the ground.

"Morning," said the worm cheerfully to Mr. Nervous.

Mr. Nervous nearly jumped out of his skin.

"What?" he shouted. "Who's there?" And then he saw the worm. "Oh, good heavens! It's a snake! Oh, dear! A man-eating snake! Oh, calamity! I'm going to be eaten alive!" And he jumped up into a tree.

"What a performance," commented the worm, and he went back into his hole.

After an hour, Mr. Nervous felt brave enough to climb down from the tree and continue his walk.

Eventually he came out of the other side of the woods and into a field.

Mr. Nervous glanced around nervously.

It was an empty field.

Or was it?

In the long grass in the middle of the field, unseen by Mr. Nervous, there was a man enjoying a nap in the autumn sunshine.

Mr. Nervous picked his way cautiously through the grass.

The man, fast asleep, snored.

"What was that?" shrieked Mr. Nervous. "It's a lion! I heard it growl! Oh, goodness gracious! Oh, dear me! A lion! A huge lion! A huge lion with enormous teeth! A huge lion with sharp teeth that's going to bite me in two! A huge, ferocious lion with enormous, sharp teeth that's going to bite me in two, if not three!"

And he fainted.

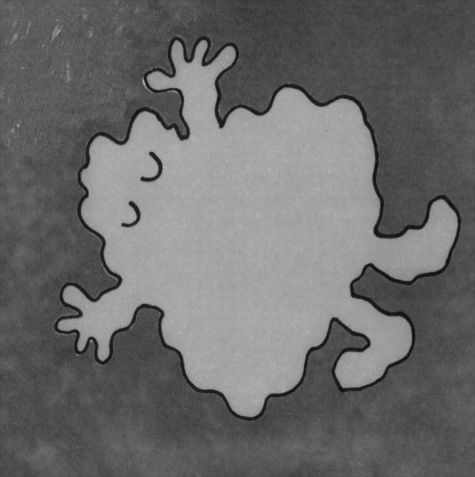

All this commotion awakened the man, who yawned, stretched, sat up, and saw Mr. Nervous lying on the ground beside him.

"Oh, dear," he said, for he was a kindly man. "Oh, dear." And he picked up Mr. Nervous and placed him gently in the palm of his hand.

Mr. Nervous came to and sat up, rubbing his eyes.

Then he saw the man's face looking at him.

"Oh, disaster!" he screamed. "Oh, calamity! It's a giant! An ogre! Oh, gracious! He's going to have me for breakfast!"

"My, my," said the man gently. "You're a nervous little chap, aren't you? What's your name?"

"Mr. N . . . N . . . N . . . N . . . N . . . N . . . Nervous," stammered Mr. Nervous.

"I used to be nervous like you," said the man, "but I learned how not to be! Would you like me to tell you the secret?"

Mr. Nervous quivered and shook and said, "Y . . . Y . . . Y . . . Y . . . Yes. P . . . P . . . P . . . Please."

"It's very simple," continued the man. "All you have to do is count up to ten, and you'll find that whatever's frightening you isn't quite so frightening after all!"

Then he set Mr. Nervous gently down on the grass.

"Remember," he said to Mr. Nervous. "Count to ten!" And off he went.

Mr. Nervous thought that it would be a very good idea if he went home immediately.

Back across the field he went. Back through the woods he went.

He was walking through the woods when he stepped on a little twig.

*Snap!* went the twig.

Mr. Nervous jumped twice his own height in terror.

"What was that?" he shrieked. "That terrible snapping noise? It's a tree falling down that's going to crush me to pieces! Oh, calamity! It's a crocodile hiding in the bushes snapping its teeth! Oh, disaster! It's . . ." And then he stopped.

He took a deep breath.

"Onetwothreefourfivesixseveneightnineten!" he said.

And he saw that what had gone *snap* was a twig. A silly old twig.

"Phew!" he said.

Mr. Nervous had almost reached his house when a leaf drifted gently down from a tree on top of him.

"Help! Police! Murder!" he screamed. "I'm being kidnapped! Oh, calamity! It's ruffians! With guns! They're going to . . ." And then he stopped.

He took a deep breath.

"Onetwothreefourfivesixseveneightnineten!"

And then he saw what had fallen on him was only a leaf. Nothing but a leaf! A stupid red leaf!

"It works," he said out loud in wonderment.

And do you know, it did work.

After that moment, Mr. Nervous was a changed man.

Well, you can see that by looking at him, can't you?

And he never shrieks, or shouts, or screams, or quivers, or shakes, or trembles anymore.

And he never hides under the bedclothes anymore.

Well.

Not very often, anyway!